The Pink Ballerina

This book belongs to:

Princess _____

gigi, God's Little Princess™
series includes:

Gigi, God's Little Princess™
(in book and DVD formats)
The Royal Tea Party
The Perfect Christmas Gift
The Pink Ballerina

And just for boys:
will, God's Mighty Warrior™
series includes:

Will, God's Mighty Warrior™
The Mystery of Magillicuddy's Gold

gigi

God's Little Princess™
The Pink Ballerina

By Sheila Walsh
Illustrated by Meredith Johnson

Tommy NELSON®

A Division of Thomas Nelson Publishers
Since 1798

www.thomasnelson.com

GIGI, GOD'S LITTLE PRINCESS™: THE PINK BALLERINA
Text © 2007 by Sheila Walsh
Illustrations © 2007 by Tommy Nelson®, a Division of Thomas Nelson, Inc.

Published in Nashville, Tennessee, by Tommy Nelson®, a Division of Thomas Nelson, Inc.

Tommy Nelson® books may be purchased in bulk for educational, business, fundraising, or sales promotional use. For information, please e-mail SpecialMarkets@ThomasNelson.com.

Scripture taken from THE MESSAGE. Copyright © 1993, 1994, 1995, 1996, 2000, 2001, 2002. Used by permission of NavPress Publishing Group.

Library of Congress Cataloging-in-Publication Data
Walsh, Sheila, 1956–
   The pink ballerina / Sheila Walsh ; illustrated by Meredith Johnson.
       p. cm. — (Gigi, God's little princess)
   Summary: Gigi and her friend Frances sign up for ballet class, thinking that is what God wants them to do.
   ISBN-13: 978-1-4003-0804-0 (hardcover)
   ISBN-10: 1-4003-0804-6 (hardcover)
[1. Ballet dancing—Fiction. 2. Christian life—Fiction.] I. Johnson, Meredith, ill. II. Title.
PZ7.W16894Pdi 2007
[E]—dc22

                                                  2006029395

Printed in China
07 08 09 10 11 LEO 5 4 3 2 1

This book is
dedicated to every
Little Princess who has
ever fallen off her shoes
or tripped over her
feather boa!

"Bye, Frances,"

Gigi called to her best friend after church.

"I'll talk to you later. I have a lot of royal thinking to do!"

"Royal thinking!" her daddy said as they drove home. "That sounds important."

"It is very important, Daddy," Gigi replied. "It *is* a royal command and it's in the Bible and it was our memory verse today and it applies particularly to princesses!"

"My goodness, take a breath, Gigi," her daddy said with a smile.

"What is your verse, Gigi?" her mommy asked.

"It's from the Pssssssalmps."

"Oh, I love the Psalms," her daddy said. "Do you know the verse by heart yet?"

"Well . . . kind of," Gigi answered as she pulled her lesson sheet out of her pocket. "It was something to do with dancing."

"What happened here?" her mommy asked.

"Well," Gigi began, "Will, who is usually not very nice to me but was nice to me today, gave me a piece of gum. I thought it would be ungodly not to take it."

"Ungodly?" her daddy asked, trying to stifle his laughter.

"Yes, but then the teacher said we were going to pray, and I thought it might be more ungodly to pray with gum in my mouth. So I tore a piece off my lesson sheet and spit my gum out and . . ."

"Oh no! This is a royal disaster!" Gigi gasped.
"I only have half the verse."

"Don't worry, Gigi," her daddy said.
"I'll find the other half for you later."

Gigi spent the rest of the day doing royal thinking.
She kept repeating the line on the paper. "I wonder
what it means?"

Let them praise his name in dance . . .

"Oh my goodness!" she squealed.
"I've got it!"

Startled, Tiara ran around the room barking.

Lord Fluffy opened one eye, muttered
something in cat language, and went
back to sleep.

"I will have to call Frances at once!" Gigi said.

"Tiara, do be quiet. This is official princess business."

"Frances, I have completed my royal thinking," Gigi began.

"You have?" Frances said, not particularly surprised.

"Yes, I have," Gigi continued. "Are you sitting down?"

"I am," Frances assured her. "I always do when you call . . . just in case."

"Frances, what do you get if you put two princesses together with a dance?" Gigi asked.

"A very small dance?" Frances suggested.

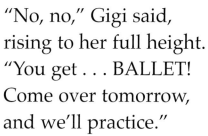

"No, no," Gigi said, rising to her full height. "You get . . . BALLET! Come over tomorrow, and we'll practice."

"Listen up, everyone," Gigi said the next day, tapping the end of her bed with a wooden spoon. "We will begin by warming up. Stretch your arms up over your head like this."

Frances and Tiara seemed willing to oblige. But Lord Fluffy was reluctant, deciding instead to pounce on Tiara's tail.

"Do you feel warm yet?" Gigi asked.

"I do," Frances replied. "Now what?"

Just then, Gigi's mommy looked in the door.
"Hmm, I think you two could use some help," she said.
"What about a ballet class?"

"What a royal idea!" Gigi said as the princess ballerinas
collapsed onto the bed.

A few days later on their way to ballet class, Gigi asked, "How many girls will be in our class?"

"I'm not sure, Gigi," her mommy said. "Miss Chambord said that it's a class for beginners."

"Well, we probably won't be in that one for long,"
Gigi said. "Frances and I have ballet in our blood,
don't we, Frances?"

"In our blood!" Frances repeated with flair.

"Welcome, la petites!" Miss Chambord said.
"We will begin by working on our poise."

"Did she say, 'Working on our noise'?"
Gigi asked.

"Poise, not noise," Frances whispered.

Miss Chambord smiled. "Poise is the way you stand.
Like so." She raised her right arm above her head.

"Now, bend your knees
and rise onto your tippytoes.
Try to be elegant like the
swan. Long necks, long necks!"

"This is killing me!" Gigi said to Frances.

And it didn't get any easier. . . .

"Bien, la petites! Now we move into the *plié*—but graceful, girls, with grace!"

"Did she ask us to say grace?" Gigi asked.

Frances rolled her eyes.

"Now, girls," Miss Chambord said, "form a circle, and we will dance around like the little butterfly."

Everything was going very well until the girl behind
Gigi stepped on the end of Gigi's feather boa.

The girls all went down like dominoes.

That night, Gigi sat on her bed. "I can't be a princess, Daddy. I just can't do it," Gigi said with big tears rolling down her cheeks.

"What do you mean, Gigi?" her daddy asked. "Of course you are a princess!"

"God won't let me be one of His princesses," Gigi cried. "I tried to dance, but I tripped everyone up with my royal pink boa! I wanted to do it perfectly and make Him proud of me."

Daddy smiled. "Gigi, you are God's little princess because He chose you, not because of anything you do or how well you do it. He looks at your heart. You can show Him that you love Him in lots of ways."

Her daddy looked around the room.
"Where is your favorite royal boa?"

"I gave it to the girl who stepped on it. She was crying because she thought it was her fault—but it wasn't really—and I wanted to make her feel better. So, I gave her the boa, and it made her smile."

"That was a kind thing to do, Gigi," her daddy said. "It makes God happy when you show kindness to others. And I think we can find you another pink feathered boa. Good night, princess."

"Good night, Daddy," Gigi said, stifling a big yawn.

Gigi lay quietly with Tiara on her tummy and Lord Fluffy on her pillow. Her daddy stepped back into her room.

"I found the rest of your verse," he said. "It's 'Let them praise his name in dance; strike up the band and make great music!'"

Suddenly, Gigi sat straight up. "That's it! We'll form a band. Just wait till Frances hears about this!"

Let them praise his name in dance; strike up
the band and make great music!
Psalm 149:3